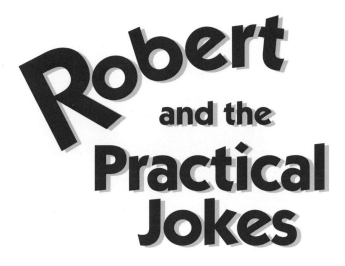

Robert
and the
Practical
Jokes

by Barbara Seuling
Illustrated by Paul Brewer

Cricket Books
Chicago

Library of Congress Cataloging-in-Publication Data

Seuling, Barbara.
    Robert and the practical jokes / by Barbara Seuling ; illustrated by Paul
Brewer.— 1st ed.
      p. cm.
    Summary: As a boys-versus-girls war of practical jokes escalates in his third-
grade classroom, Robert finds it difficult to ask a girl's help in learning to dance in
time for a family wedding reception.
ISBN-13: 978-0-8126-2741-1
ISBN-10: 0-8126-2741-5

    [1. Practical jokes—Fiction. 2. Schools—Fiction. 3. Sex role—Fiction.
4. Dancing—Fiction.] I. Brewer, Paul, 1950- ill. II. Title.
    PZ7.S5135Rpm 2006
    [Fic]—dc22

                             2005025411

For the real Lindsey Ilana
—B. S.

For Dianne Harrell
—P. B.

Contents

A Bloodcurdling
Scream

"AIIIEEEEE-EEE-EEEE!"

You'd think someone was being murdered. Nobody screamed like Melissa Thurm. Not even that woman in the *King Kong* movie when she was picked up by the giant gorilla.

Mrs. Bernthal spun around at the sound and walked right over to the table where Melissa had been sitting. She picked up the rubber snake and asked, "Whose is this?"

1

Robert gulped and raised his hand. "It's . . . mine," he said in a small voice.

"I see," said Mrs. Bernthal, walking back to her desk with the snake dangling from two fingers. She opened the middle drawer of the desk and dropped the snake in. Everybody knew that once something went into that drawer, you never saw it again. Kevin Kransky's plastic vomit went in it last week, and just yesterday, Mrs. Bernthal added Lester's shrunken head when he was caught dangling it in front of Emily during journal writing.

Robert felt as if his heart had dropped into his stomach. That snake had cost him four dollars. He'd had to get an advance on his allowance for three whole weeks to buy it.

It wasn't his fault, either. Lester Willis had grabbed Robert's snake off the desk as he was showing it to Paul, then ran over

2

and dropped it in front of Melissa. Robert could only watch in horror as Melissa shrieked and jumped up, knocking over her chair.

Paul Felcher, Robert's best friend, looked at him miserably from across the table.

"Children," said Mrs. Bernthal, "the practical jokes have gone far enough. It's time you learned something from the experience." She looked directly at Robert.

"But I didn't—" he started to say.

Mrs. Bernthal did not let him finish.

"Class, I want you to add something to your homework." There were groans from all over the room. "Write ten interesting facts about snakes."

There went Robert's chance to watch TV or play with Huckleberry in the yard. He probably wouldn't even have time to sleep.

"Melissa," added Mrs. Bernthal, "you may be excused from this assignment. As a matter of fact, you may help me mark the homework."

"No fair!" said Kevin Kransky. That's what Robert was thinking, too.

"Well, Kevin, then you can add another

page to tell us why this is unfair." There were a few uncomfortable giggles.

"Yeah, Barf Brain," shouted Lester.

"And Lester," said Mrs. Bernthal, "you can add five additional facts to your list."

For the first time that day, Robert saw Melissa smile.

Extra Homework

"**T**hanks a lot, Robert," said Susanne Lee Rodgers, passing Robert in the schoolyard. "Because of you, we have extra homework."

Kristi Mills was right beside her, wearing an angry face.

"It wasn't my fault!" said Robert.

Susanne Lee sucked her teeth and followed Kristi over to a cluster of girls who were jumping rope.

Nobody even cared that Robert wasn't the one who'd scared Melissa, or that his great souvenir from the reptile exhibit at the Bronx Zoo this past weekend was gone forever.

Lester, just a short distance away, must have heard his name mentioned. He came over as Kristi and Susanne Lee walked away. "You talking about me?" he asked.

"Yeah, about how you got us extra homework," Robert said. He would have liked telling Lester off, but he was still unsure about Lester. He might go ballistic and go back to being a bully and try to beat him up.

"Girls are such sissies," said Lester.

"We are not sissies!" said Vanessa Nicolini, stopping short as she passed him. "How can you blame it on us? How would you like it if someone dropped a snake in front of you?"

"I'd laugh," said Lester. "I'm not a scaredy-cat."

That was probably true. Robert didn't think much scared Lester. Except maybe Lucy Ritts. And who should walk up to them just then but Lucy herself.

"So, Lester, how does it feel to be the class knucklehead?"

Robert had never heard that term before. It sounded like something his mom or dad might say. Leave it to Lucy to come up with it. She'd joined Mrs. Bernthal's class only a couple of weeks ago, when her family moved into the neighborhood. Already, she had the reputation of being fearless.

"Oh yeah, Monster Girl?" he said. Lester had nicknamed her that the minute he saw her. Lucy was not only bigger than the other girls, she was good at sports and could stand up for herself.

"And what are the big bad girls going to do?" Lester kept badgering her. "Call me names? Oh, I'm so worried."

"Lester," she said, "you won't be laughing when the girls get even with you."

Oh no. Why does Lester say and do such stupid things? Robert wished there were a way to turn Lester off, like an annoying alarm clock.

Ten Facts

After school, Robert sat on the living room floor, leafing through the *Family Encyclopedia,* looking up snakes. Huck lay next to him, watching every move.

Robert already knew something about snakes. He had read a book about them when he became the class snake monitor. He knew snakes could live about a week without eating. He knew they were cold-blooded and had to stay warm or they could die.

That was only two facts. He needed eight more. He scratched Huck's belly. The dog's back leg thumped with pleasure.

The encyclopedia had information on the most poisonous snakes, and about people in India who hunted them to get their venom.

Robert learned about the smallest snakes and harmless snakes you could find in your own backyard.

When he had seven facts on his list, he was stuck. Where else had he read about snakes? Oh! Right. His Weird & Wacky Facts books.

Robert put the encyclopedia back in the bookcase and went upstairs. Huck followed right behind. Robert looked through six Weird & Wacky books before he found a fact about snakes. It said that some snakes have fangs that fold back on hinges when they're not being used. That was cool.

Robert found another fact, that sometimes a snake is born with two heads. The two heads fight over food even though it

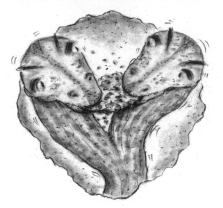

goes into one stomach that they share. And if they get really angry, they try to swallow each other.

"No way!" he said out loud. Huck lifted his head for a moment, then lowered it again.

He needed one more fact about snakes. Tapping his pencil, he thought hard until it came to him. He wrote:

They have a World of Reptiles at the Bronx Zoo and a souvenir shop where you can buy a fake snake for four dollars.

By the time he was through, he knew more about snakes than he ever wanted to know. "Come on, Huck." Robert got up. He had to take the list to his dad to look at.

Robert's dad wanted to see his homework every night.

Robert winced as his dad wrote something on the paper. Lifting his pen, he asked, "You weren't going to hand in this paper, were you?" Robert felt his dad staring at him and knew what he had to answer.

"No," he said. "I was going to write it over on a clean page."

"That's good," said his dad. Robert's dad was a neat freak. He even lined up all the jars in the refrigerator door by size. Of course he would expect Robert to do his paper over if it had a lot of eraser marks on it.

"That's pretty interesting information, Tiger," said his dad. He handed the paper back to Robert.

"Thanks," Robert answered. He went upstairs and copied his snake facts onto a clean notebook page. This time he spelled "stomach" correctly.

As he got into his pajamas, Robert thought about the *Instant Millionaire* show. He had missed it because of all his homework. As he brushed his teeth, he looked in the mirror, imagining himself as a contestant on the show. He imagined the emcee looking very much like his dad.

"And now, Robert, for one million dollars, can you tell us ten interesting facts about snakes?" the emcee asked.

Huck barked. It sounded to Robert like, "Sure you can!"

Back in the classroom the next day, Robert went to check on Sally, the real snake, who was their class pet. She lived in a glass tank. Paul, the best artist in the class, had painted her name on the front of the tank. Robert had brought in a small piece of a tree branch that Sally liked to hide under.

Robert loved Sally. He thought snakes

were beautiful. He reached in to stroke Sally.

"Can I touch her?"

Robert was surprised to see Lucy standing there.

"Sure," he said. He was even more surprised when Lucy picked up Sally. Not too many kids wanted to handle Sally. Most of them thought snakes were slimy. Not Robert. He knew Sally's skin was dry and smooth.

"She's beautiful," said Lucy. Robert watched Sally make an "S" curve as Lucy stroked her. That made Robert feel better, because that meant Sally was happy.

"Too bad about the other snake," she said.

"Yeah," said Robert. "Thanks." Lucy was the only person besides Paul who hadn't gotten angry with him over the snake episode. Was she really planning revenge on Lester?

Lester came up to them by the snake tank. Robert expected him to say something annoying to Lucy, but Lester surprised him.

"My dad was almost bitten by a rattlesnake once," he said.

"Really?" asked Robert.

"Yeah, when he was in the army," Lester said. "He was in the desert in Texas. A rattlesnake tried to bite him, but my dad had thick army boots on, and they saved him."

"Wow," said Lucy. All thoughts about revenge seemed to have been forgotten.

The morning passed quietly, and Mrs. Bernthal asked them to write in their journals as she marked their homework papers.

Over at Table Five, Melissa marked papers, too.

When the bell rang for lunch, they went to the cafeteria. Robert sat down with Paul, Kevin, and Brian Hoberman at a lunch table. Robert took out his sandwich and opened it. Bologna. Cool. He pulled out the bologna and bit into it.

"Lester, that's not funny!" he heard.

Looking up, Robert saw Lester over at the girls' table showing them a mouthful of chewed food.

Mrs. Bernthal was way over on the other side of the lunchroom. She had lunchroom duty today and walked around as they ate.

"Lester, you're disgusting, not funny," said Susanne Lee. Other kids were laughing, even some of the girls.

"That should improve their appetites," said Brian, as Lester came over to the boys' table and sat down.

"It's so easy to gross them out," said Lester, grinning.

Robert didn't know why seeing chewed food was so funny, but he was used to his brother, Charlie, doing it at home when their parents weren't looking. And he always laughed. He couldn't help it.

Susanne Lee glowered at the boys, but at least she didn't cry or squeal or get hysterical, like Melissa.

Lucy walked by their table a little later on the way to dump her tray. She turned and displayed a wide-open mouth full of chewed spaghetti. The boys cracked up.

Robert looked around. Mrs. Bernthal was looking his way. Had she seen him laughing with his mouth full of bologna? Would she think he was making trouble again?

The Mouse

In the gym, Robert did his best to hide when teams were chosen for a softball game. He knew he was a terrible hitter and an even worse catcher.

"What's up?" said Lucy, finding him behind the equipment stacked on the bench.

"Oh. Nothing," said Robert.

"You've got to play, you know. Might as well get it over with." She sat down next to him. "I've seen you play. You don't know how to catch," she said.

"Thanks. I already know that," said Robert.

"I can help you. There's a way to hang on to the ball when it hits your hand."

Robert listened more attentively.

"The ball usually comes in on a bounce from the batter to you. Keep your glove open and ready for it. Don't run into it, just let it come to you. When it hits your glove, scoop up the ball as you move back. Squeeze your glove around it, and keep your hand facing up, not down, or the ball will fall out of the glove."

Robert listened, but he wasn't sure. He was bad enough at ball playing without doing anything that could make him look even worse. But he didn't exactly have much to lose.

"Thanks," he said.

Lucy smiled and got up. "Sure," she said as she went off to join her team.

The game started. Robert was on team

number two. They had to take him—he was the last one left.

It was his turn to bat. Get it over with. That's all he could do. He walked up to the plate and held the bat the way he thought he was supposed to. It seemed to wobble. He tightened his grip.

The ball came in a low pitch. He swung at it and missed. The next ball was too high, and it was followed by one that was too low, but Robert swung at both of them. He was out. He went back to the bench.

When the teams switched places, he got up to take his position in the back of the gym. Kids rarely hit the ball there, and that's why they gave him that spot.

Lucy, on the other team, was up at bat. She hit the ball with a smack that sent it his way. It bounced toward him, and he concentrated on being ready, with the

glove open. When the ball hit, he scooped it up, moving back. He squeezed his fingers slightly around the ball, holding it up, not down. He caught the ball! His team let out a whoop. Lucy was safe on first base. She glanced over at Robert and gave him a thumbs-up sign.

Robert wished his brother, Charlie, could have seen him. The only thing Robert did better than Charlie in sports was snowboarding, and that was only because Robert had been on a snowboard and Charlie hadn't—yet.

Robert hardly saw the rest of the game. He kept thinking of how good it felt to catch the ball. He never wanted to be an athlete, like Charlie, but he enjoyed being able to help his team win. This gave him hope.

After gym, the class was working on math problems when suddenly Andy Liskin cried, "A mouse! A mouse!"

Furniture scraped the floor, kids ran everywhere, and Melissa climbed up on a chair, screaming at the top of her lungs.

Mrs. Bernthal looked up from her math book, her face red.

"It went that way," said Andy, pointing to the teacher's coat closet. Robert had seen it, too.

Mrs. Bernthal snapped the book closed.

"Take your seats," she said firmly. "You, too, Melissa." Melissa got down and sat at her desk, sniffling.

"We cannot keep having the class disrupted," Mrs. Bernthal said.

"But the mouse . . ." Andy said.

"That will be enough, Andrew. I think you're carrying the practical jokes too far."

Uh-oh. Mrs. Bernthal was really mad now. She wasn't even listening to Andy, who never got into trouble. Andy looked crushed.

"Judging by what I've collected from you over the past few weeks," she continued, "you enjoy the strange, the odd . . ." She opened the desk drawer and looked in. ". . . and the truly gross." She had a weird look on her face, like maybe she had smelled something bad.

"Our next project was going to be Ocean Life, but instead, we are going to have one that will give you plenty of opportunity to study the ghastly subjects that fascinate you so much." As she spoke, she printed words on the chalkboard:

The Weird and Horrible

"What does that mean?" asked Emily Asher. She almost never called out.

"This will be your next project," said Mrs. Bernthal. "It includes whatever strange, bizarre, unusual things interest you. Maybe studying these topics will, once and for all, satisfy your morbid curiosity."

"Cool," said Lester.

Morbid? Robert thought he knew what morbid meant. It was something about death. He wondered what they would have to do. He hoped he wouldn't have to look at a dead person.

Robert's mom and dad had gone to the funeral of an elderly uncle once and asked if he wanted to come, but when he found out he might have to look at his dead relative, Robert said no.

"You may choose any topic you wish, no matter how weird or horrible, as long as you research it thoroughly. We'll listen to your presentations next week, starting Monday. The earlier you bring them in, the better."

"Will we get extra credit for bringing them in early?" asked Susanne Lee.

"No, but you will get it over with faster," said Mrs. Bernthal.

"I'm choosing Lester Willis for my topic," said Kristi. "He's gross and he's disgusting. And this whole thing is his fault!" Everyone laughed. Mrs. Bernthal tapped her ruler, but even she smiled.

Robert looked at Mrs. Bernthal. Had she heard what Kristi said? It *was* Lester's fault. He couldn't tell her himself or he'd be a snitch, but there it was. Kristi had told her.

A Really Weird Project

"**C**an I do shrunken heads?" Lester called out.

"*May* I do shrunken heads," Mrs. Bernthal said.

"Sure you can, but I want to do them, too," said Lester.

The class cracked up.

"I'm glad we have a comedian in the class, Lester. We all love to laugh. Perhaps you will put on a performance for us when we're finished with our projects. Yes, you may do shrunken heads. Research the topic thoroughly and tell us all about it." Mrs. Bernthal sat down again and opened a book.

"What about plastic vomit?" asked Joey Rizzo, looking at Kevin. The class broke into laughter.

"Yes," said Mrs. Bernthal, making a face. "That would be acceptable." The children looked shocked.

Andy raised his hand.

"Yes, Andrew?"

"Mrs. Bernthal, a mouse . . ."

"Yes, Andrew," Mrs. Bernthal said, remaining calm, "but mice are actually quite harmless and cute. Surely you can think of something more weird or horrible than mice."

"No, I meant . . ."

"That's quite all right, Andrew. You may

choose mice. Many people think mice are disgusting. I'll be interested to hear in your report why this is so."

Robert saw Andy slouch down in his seat.

Mrs. Bernthal put on her glasses and opened the book. "We are up to chapter six of *James and the Giant Peach*," she said, and she began to read. She read to them every Friday afternoon.

Robert tried to listen, but his mind wandered several times. At last the bell rang, and everyone scrambled to leave. As Robert joined the line to file out, he saw Mrs. Bernthal opening her closet to get her coat.

"AAAAAAAH!" she cried, jumping back. A small gray mouse darted out and ran out the door and down the hall.

"I tried to tell her," said Andy.

"Yeah, I know," said Robert.

It was really awful when someone thought you did something you didn't do.

weeeawobbel

Morbid Curiosity

"**H**ey, Huckleberry," said Robert, coming in the door. His dog always gave him a huge welcome, with wet sloppy kisses and a wagging tail.

"Hi, Rob," his mom called to him from the kitchen.

"Hi," said Robert.

"Something wrong?" His mom came out to see.

Robert wiggled away from Huckleberry so he could ease out of his backpack. "No. It's just . . . Mrs. Bernthal gave us a weird project."

"What do you mean, weird?" his mom asked.

"I mean, it's not the kind of project that teachers give you."

"Why? What is it?" asked his mom.

Robert shrugged. "It's about weird stuff. Even shrunken heads and plastic vomit."

Mrs. Dorfman's eyebrows went up. "Are you sure?"

Robert nodded his head. "Yes, I'm sure. Mrs. Bernthal calls it 'The Weird and Horrible.' She said those topics would be acceptable."

"Well, I'm sure she had a very good reason," said his mom. But Robert could tell she was wondering about it, too. She even brought it up over dinner.

It was Friday. That meant they ate pizza and watched a movie together. Charlie was looking through the four DVDs their dad had brought in for the weekend.

Robert had cut up a slice of pizza with lots of pepperoni on it for Huckleberry and had just taken his first gooey bite of his own slice, when his mom made her announcement.

"Robert has quite an interesting class project," she said. "It's about weird and disgusting things."

Robert's mouth was full of pizza. "Weeeawobbel," he said.

"Oh, right. Weird and horrible things," his mom said.

Charlie looked up from the DVDs. "That's cool!" he said.

"He can choose any subject, no matter how—er—bizarre," his mom continued, shuddering. "Why do you suppose Mrs. Bernthal would do that?"

"I don't know," said Robert's dad. "What do you think, Tiger?"

Robert shrugged. "I don't know. I think she's punishing us." He held up his slice of pizza and took another bite.

"Why? What did you do?" asked his dad.

He couldn't tell them about the snake. They might believe he was to blame, too. "Lester brought in a shrunken head," he said.

Charlie snorted as he tried to laugh and chew at the same time.

"And Kevin Kransky brought in plastic vomit," Robert added.

Robert's mom made a face and put down her pizza.

"Sounds like reverse psychology to me," said Robert's mom. She poured herself some soda.

"What's that?" asked Robert.

"Doing just the opposite of what's expected," said Charlie. He turned to his mom. "Right?"

His mom nodded. "Yes, Charlie. It helps to turn things around sometimes."

"I was into horror movies as a kid," said Robert's dad.

"You still are," Robert's mom reminded him.

"Well, yes. A fascination for things that are strange or different is normal."

"What does 'morbid' mean?" asked Robert.

"Morbid? That means gruesome or grim," said Robert's dad. "Why?"

"Mrs. Bernthal says we have a morbid curiosity."

"She's got that right," said his dad.

Charlie slid the disc into the DVD player, and they sat back to enjoy the movie: *The Night of the Mummies.*

Is It Strange Enough?

"**L**ook at this! You can make your own slime!" said Robert, sitting at the computer in Paul's room. Paul came to look at the screen. It was a kids' science Web site on lots of yucky topics.

"Cool," said Paul. "So . . . are you choosing slime as your topic?"

"No," Robert said, clicking the mouse. Another page came up, all about insects. He read about flies and how they see a gazillion different things at the same time. That just made him feel itchy. Besides, he didn't know if it was strange enough for his project. He clicked again.

Paul took over for a while and found a page on blood and guts, on a Web site about the human body. There was a demonstration of how a wound healed. Robert was beginning to feel queasy.

It was halfway through Saturday morning. They needed a break.

"This is hard," said Paul. "I can't make up my mind. Nothing seems right. Maybe that's because it feels like we're only fooling around instead of doing a school project."

"My dad says it's normal to be interested in strange and creepy stuff."

Paul laughed. "Yeah, your dad would say that. Remember Halloween?"

How could he forget? Robert's dad always went nuts at Halloween and decorated the house with witchy, creepy things from his horror collection. He even played scary tricks on him and Charlie and their friends.

"Nobody does Halloween like your dad," said Paul. Robert agreed with that.

Robert thought of the boxes of masks, costumes, makeup, fake spiders, cobwebs, vampire teeth, and other toys and tricks that came out of thc Dorfman attic every Halloween.

"That's it!" he said. "We should look in my dad's collection!"

Robert's dad was a master at this horror stuff. Why hadn't Robert thought of it before?

They walked briskly back to Robert's

house to ask his dad if they could look through his horror collection.

"Well, if it's for educational purposes . . ." he teased. He climbed the pull-down ladder into the attic and brought down two boxes. They opened them in the living room.

"Just be careful with these," said Robert's dad, "and let me know if you want to borrow anything."

"Thanks, Dad," said Robert. He and Paul spent the rest of the morning looking at— and trying out—some of the items. Robert liked the crawling hand best, and they laughed when he put it inside a paper bag, turned it on, and watched it crawl out.

Robert's mom made tomato-and-cheese sandwiches for lunch, and they ate them while they watched a couple of movies from the collection: first, *The Island of the Living Dead*, about zombies, and then *The*

Wolf Man, with Lon Chaney. Robert had seen the movies before, but this time, he really wondered about werewolves. Were they real?

When the movie was over, he said to Paul, "I think I know what my topic is."

Paul looked a little disappointed. "What?" he asked.

"Werewolves."

Paul broke out in a big grin. "Great!" he said. "I was afraid you were going to say horror films. That's what I want to do!"

With a hoot, they gave each other a high-five. They had their topics!

Shrunken Heads and Werewolves

On Monday morning, Susanne Lee started off The Weird and Horrible presentations. She brought in a chart showing the different parts of an eyeball and taped it to the chalkboard.

"This is not really disgusting," she said. "Doctors have to do it all the time." She looked in Lester's direction. "But I know some of you will find it gross."

She walked over to the reading table, picked up a package wrapped in butcher's paper, and opened it. "This is a sheep's eyeball," she announced.

The children leaned forward or stood up to see. Melissa gasped and stayed in her seat.

"You can come closer," said Susanne Lee. Boys and girls clustered around the table as she pulled on a pair of rubber gloves. Melissa stayed put.

Susanne Lee opened a small kit with tools inside. "This is a dissecting knife," she said. Robert thought he heard a small squeal from Melissa. The knife in Susanne Lee's hand had a small blade at the end of a long handle. There were a few gagging sounds from the group around the table, and Maggie went back to her table and sat down.

Susanne Lee proceeded to cut apart the eyeball, naming the corresponding parts on the chart.

"That was very good, Susanne Lee," said Mrs. Bernthal, looking a little pale. "I'm glad you didn't do your demonstration just before lunch."

Vanessa followed with a report on a shark that was found to have a lot of strange things in its stomach, including an alarm clock, a rubber boot, an electric fan, and a rubber tube. Kristi did hers on an ancient Chinese empress who let her fingernails grow two feet long. She had to have servants do everything for her because she kept her hands on pillows all day so her nails wouldn't break. Joey told them about body snatchers, people who stole bodies out of graves and sold them to medical students, who would then cut up the bodies to study anatomy—the bones and muscles of the body.

Paul's talk, on horror movies, had everyone's attention, especially when he got to the part about how some of the special effects were done.

"This is the *Frankenstein* monster," he said. He held up pictures of the familiar character, played by Boris Karloff. "The makeup for him was created by a man named Jack Pierce. It was so unique that it was copyrighted, so nobody else could use it." He passed the pictures around.

"My favorite horror movie of all is *Dracula,* because even though it's an old movie in black and white, it's better than most movies in color, and the blood looks even scarier in black than it would in red." He held up more pictures, of Dracula in his castle and Dracula ready to attack a victim.

Suddenly, blood seemed to spill out of Paul's mouth, dribbling down his chin.

"Mrs. Bernthal! He's bleeding!" cried Vanessa, jumping up.

Mrs. Bernthal ran over to Paul, but just in time, he spit something into his hand and held it up.

"It's fake," he said. "Like in the movies."

"That's a relief," said Mrs. Bernthal.

"This is how they make blood come out of people's mouths after they are shot in the movies," Paul explained. "You put this little capsule of red liquid under your tongue," he said, "then, after you're shot, you bite down on it and it breaks."

Paul wiped off the red liquid and finished his report. Mrs. Bernthal told him his demonstration was excellent.

Nobody was surprised when Lester did his report on shrunken heads, but everyone was surprised that he knew so much about them. In some parts of the world, he said, people used to cut off the heads of their enemies and sew up the lips so that evil spirits couldn't come out. Then they shrunk the heads with a special smoking process.

"I would show you a fake shrunken head, but I don't have it anymore," Lester said, looking over at Mrs. Bernthal.

"I think everyone knows what it looks like, Lester. Good job. You may sit down."

Robert still thought shrunken heads were grotesque, but now they didn't seem as scary as they once were. Emily Asher's report on dung beetles, creatures that lived in the poop of other animals, was mild by comparison.

He asked to be excused when Brian got up to talk about cockroaches. He didn't mind missing that.

In the boys' room, he worked fast. He opened a tube of glue that he had in his pocket. He squeezed some onto the back of his right hand. Then, carefully, he pressed on strands of fake fur, from his other pocket, a little at a time. He was starting to sweat. Mrs. Bernthal might wonder what he was up to, so he put on the last of the fur in a clump and went back to the classroom.

When it was Robert's turn, he nodded at Paul, picked up his page of notes with his left hand, and walked up to the front of the room.

"In the olden days, people believed in lots of strange ideas," he said. "That's because they didn't know much, so they made up stories to explain things that happened. So if a child disappeared, or someone was murdered, they believed it could be a werewolf—a person who changed shape from human to wolf and then attacked. Thousands of people in France were accused of being werewolves, and some of them were executed. You could be one of them if you happened to be very hairy."

Robert stopped for a breath. He took his right hand out of his pocket and pretended to brush something off his cheek.

"Look!" cried Paul. "Robert is turning into a werewolf!"

Lester stood up to see.

Robert had everyone's attention now.

"People all over the world—even Native Americans—believed in some kind of creature like a werewolf. A lot of movies were made about werewolves, because people are fascinated by the unusual."

"How did you do that?" said Lucy, pointing to his hand.

"My dad has a theatrical makeup kit that he uses for Halloween," said Robert. "I asked if I could use it to look like a werewolf for my report. It was too much work and too expensive to cover my whole body, so I just did one hand."

"Is it real fur?" asked Abby Ranko.

"No, it's fake. It's what actors use when they need to have mustaches or beards. You stick it on with spirit gum, a kind of glue."

"That was quite illuminating, Robert," said Mrs. Bernthal. Robert knew that must mean she liked it. "Settle down now, class. We'll go to lunch in a few minutes. When we come back, we'll finish up the reports."

Sweet Revenge

There were more reports, on warts, Siamese twins, someone who could touch her forehead with her tongue, and people who filed their teeth to points to look beautiful.

Lucy was the last to share her topic. It was about unusual food.

"In China," she said, "people eat eggs that have been buried for a hundred years." There were sounds of disgust around the room.

Lucy went on. "At a wedding feast in the Middle East, you might be served chicken that was baked inside a goat, that was baked inside a camel. And in Africa, fried grasshoppers are considered a treat."

"Eeee-yew!" cried Maggie.

Robert felt his stomach flip. He could picture the grasshoppers hopping in the pan. How could anyone eat stuff like that?

Lucy held up a can of reindeer meatballs from Finland and a package of dried seaweed from Japan. Robert noticed everyone wrinkled their noses. He did, too.

He watched in fascination as Lucy put down the meatballs and seaweed and opened a box.

"I'm going to pass around these chocolate treats," she said, handing the box to Brian, who was nearest to her. He took the box eagerly. "They are genuine, chocolate-covered worms from Mexico."

"Eeeeee-ew!" Brian quickly passed the box to Abby Ranko, who sat across from him at Table Two.

"No thanks. I've already got one," she said, waving a wiggly chocolate candy at him.

"Me, too," said Pamela Rose, waving the box away. She showed her chocolate worm.

Brian shoved the box at Matt. Matt read the label on the box and quickly passed it to Emily at the next table.

"They're for real!" Matt said, making a face. "I thought she was kidding."

The box went around the room. The girls were smiling and munching on their chocolate worms, while the boys were clearly grossed out.

"What's the matter, boys?" asked Kristi, moving the box along to Lester. "Are you too scared to eat a tiny little worm?"

"They're sooooooo good," said Susanne Lee, licking her lips.

"Come on, Lester, you big baby," said Lucy. The boys egged him on. Lester looked a little green as he took a worm and let it dangle for a moment. Then he threw it back in the box. The class roared with laughter.

"Lester isn't so tough after all. Why don't you guys try one?" Susanne Lee pushed the box at Kevin, then at Joey.

"Yeah, who's a sissy now?" asked Vanessa.

None of the boys would touch the chocolate-covered worms. When the box came to Robert, he stared into it for a moment. It looked just like chocolate candy, except he knew it wasn't. There were real worms inside. And the girls seemed to be enjoying them.

The girls kept after him. "Take one, Robert. It's really gooooood." That was Kristi. Finally, rather than listen to all the cheering and jeering, he picked one out of the box, closed his eyes, held his nose, and swallowed it. The children were silent as they watched him. All he could taste was the chocolate.

"Not bad," he said.

When the box came back to Lucy, she closed it and went back to her seat.

"Thank you, Lucy," said Mrs. Bernthal. She congratulated them all. "You have certainly chosen some interesting subjects. I learned a great deal, and I hope you did, too."

Robert wasn't sure what he had learned, but he had eaten a worm! He felt proud of himself. His dad must have been right. It was O.K. to be curious about things that were strange.

Mrs. Bernthal tapped her ruler. The class came to attention.

"You have shown yourselves to be mature in your choices of topics and your presentations. And for that, you may have your confiscated items back." A cheer went up from several of the boys. Mrs. Bernthal opened the desk drawer and called them up one at a time. Robert thought his heart would beat right out of his chest when she called his name.

Afternoon Snack

As they filed out of school at three o'clock, Lucy caught up to Robert.

"Here," she said. "Take these." She offered him the box of chocolate worms.

"N-n-no thanks," said Robert.

"You said you liked them."

"They were O.K. But I don't think I want any more."

"Really? What am I going to do with these?" she said. "They're gross. I only got them for my report."

"I thought you and the other girls liked them," said Robert.

"Sure, but ours didn't have real worms in them."

"What?"

Lucy laughed. "We made ours yesterday at Kristi's house."

Robert felt like he'd been punched in the stomach. "What about the one I ate?"

"That one was the real thing. I told you we'd get even." Lucy thrust the box of chocolate-covered worms at him and ran off, laughing, to join the other girls.

Robert was barely in the house when Huckleberry came bounding toward him. He bent over to pet the dog, calling out, "Mom, I got my snake back!" As soon as he could get free, he rushed to the kitchen.

"I didn't know your snake was missing," his mom said, washing an apple under the faucet and greeting him with a smile.

Oops! How could he be so dumb? He had never told her about the rubber snake episode. Maybe he would do that tonight, along with some juicy stories from the class project. It was time to spill it all out. But right now, he wanted to play with Huckleberry.

"Oh, I almost forgot," he said, showing the box of chocolate-covered worms to his mom.

She looked at the box and made a face. "Oh my!" she said. "Are these really worms?"

"Yup. Lucy gave them to me," Robert said. "They were part of her report on unusual foods. You don't have to eat them. I just brought them home to show you. She didn't want them."

"Why did she give them to you?"

"Because I ate one, and nobody else did."

"You *ate* one?" asked his mom, her eyebrows as high as they could go.

Robert nodded as he put the box on the counter. He'd show them later, when he told them all about The Weird and Horrible presentations.

"Come on," he said to Huckleberry.

Robert had just put his hand on the doorknob when Charlie came rushing in.

"Hey," he called as he swept through the kitchen to the fridge and took out a Snapple. He saw the chocolates on the counter, opened the box without looking first, and helped himself. As he ran upstairs, munching, Robert and his mom stared in horror, then cracked up.

Birthday Boy

Sunday was Robert's birthday. He had almost forgotten about it. Nine sounded a lot older than eight, but so far, he felt the same. His mom had made his favorite dinner: hamburgers and french fries, smothered in catsup. Now it was time to open his presents.

"Open mine first," said his brother, Charlie, handing him a package the size of a shoebox wrapped in blue-and-yellow-striped paper. Robert tore it open. It was a model Tyrannosaurus rex.

"The arms move, and its eyes light up," said Charlie, grinning.

"Thanks!" said Robert. This would be a great addition to his dinosaur collection. Sometimes, Charlie could be really nice.

Robert put it on the floor and turned the switch to ON. The dinosaur started to move.

Huckleberry growled and backed away as the dinosaur advanced, step by step, toward him. Cautiously, he approached it again and sniffed its tail. They all laughed.

"Dogs will be dogs," said Mr. Dorfman.

"Open the silver one," said his mom, pointing to another package, wrapped in silver paper with a blue bow stuck on top. Robert shook it, read the tag, then tore it open.

"It's the *Star Wars* action figure I wanted!" he cried. "Thanks, Mom! Thanks, Dad!"

"You're welcome," said his mom.

"Sure thing, Tiger," said his dad.

There was a card from Grandma Dorfman in Florida with a twenty-dollar bill inside. "Cool," he said. He could sure use the money. He had been broke since he'd bought that rubber snake.

The last present was from Grandma Judy. Her card said, "This does everything except cook and wash windows." Grandma Judy was funny. It was a wrist watch. The box said it told the time all over the world, showed the year, month, and day, and even reminded you of important appointments.

"Wow," he said, putting it on. He would figure out how to set it later.

"Happy birthday to you, happy birthday to you . . ."

Everyone sang as Robert's mom brought out a birthday cake with ten lighted candles on it, one for each year plus one to grow on. Robert joined in at the end, almost in tune, "Happy birthday to meeeeeee."

"Make a wish, birthday boy," said his mom.

Robert closed his eyes, made a wish, and blew. When he opened his eyes, the candles were still lit. He tried again, taking a bigger breath this time. The candles were still burning. Charlie laughed.

"Yo, Rob, what kind of lungs do you have?"

Robert tried again, but the candles still didn't go out. By now Charlie was laughing

so hard, Robert knew his brother was up
to something.

"They're trick candles!" said Robert.

Charlie acted like he thought that was
the funniest thing he ever saw. His mom and

dad laughed, too. That Charlie! Robert still fell for his tricks every time. Charlie was probably paying him back for the chocolate worms. He had eaten almost the whole box before he read the label and upchucked.

His mom found the regular candles and replaced the trick ones with real ones. As she lit the candles, Robert made a new birthday wish: He wished his brother would realize he wasn't a dumb little kid anymore.

The World's Worst Wrist Watch

Two pieces of birthday cake! No wonder Robert felt stuffed. Upstairs, he flopped down on his beanbag chair. Huckleberry lay sleeping beside him. Robert took his new action figure out of its wrapping and played with it. Then he started the dinosaur and watched it go.

Finally, he got to his watch. The instructions were hard to follow and in teeny-tiny print. He couldn't figure out how to set the time.

Robert thumped downstairs.

69

"Dad?" he asked.

"What is it, Tiger?" asked Mr. Dorfman, looking up from his newspaper.

"I can't set my watch." Robert's dad loved anything to do with numbers, so Robert thought it was a good idea to ask him.

"There's no such word as 'can't,'" he said.

"Huh?"

"Never say 'I can't,'" said his dad, "or you will believe it and then you won't even try."

Uh-oh. This could be one of those times when his dad felt like teaching him something important. His dad was smart and all, but sometimes Robert just wanted a little bit of help, and he got a whole lesson instead.

"O.K.," said Robert. He handed his watch to his dad, along with the instructions that came with it.

Mr. Dorfman took the watch and the instructions, but he looked at Robert. "I think you don't believe me," he said.

"I . . . I do," said Robert. He didn't really know what else to say.

"Get the dictionary," said Mr. Dorfman.

Robert wished by now that he had asked his mom to set the watch, instead. If she didn't know how to set the time, she would just say so and be done with it. He went over to the bookcase and pulled out the dictionary. He brought it over to his dad and put it on the coffee table.

"Open it," said his dad. "Look up the word 'can't.'"

Robert did as he was told. He flipped to the C's: candy—cannibal—canoe . . .

"Somebody wrote in this book!" said Robert. There was a black line through the word "can't." He was surprised. His mom told him never ever to write in a book unless it was meant to be written in.

"I did that," said his dad. Robert looked at him like he couldn't believe it. "That's how strongly I believe in what I just said."

Wow. His dad meant business if he wrote in a book. He wondered if his mom knew.

"Dad . . . ?" said Robert.

"Yes, Tiger?"

"Um . . . my watch. Can you make it tell the time?"

His father looked at the watch again and at the instructions. Then he pressed some buttons, made it beep a few times, and handed it back to Robert.

"There you go," he said. "Date and time." That was good enough for Robert. He didn't need to know the rest, like what time it was in Australia. He wanted to leave before his dad thought of something else to teach him.

"Thanks," said Robert.

"You're welcome," said his father, going back to his newspaper.

Mrs. Dorfman came in as Robert was putting the dictionary back on the shelf.

"We got an invitation in the mail today—to cousin Heather's wedding," she said. Robert remembered cousin Heather. She was pretty, with long blond hair, and once she'd told him he was handsome. Of course, he was only four years old at the time.

"That's nice," said his dad.

"We'll have to get you a suit, Robert," said his mom. "You can wear your new watch and be really spiffy."

Robert groaned. Spiffy was a mom word. He hated being spiffy. He hated shopping, and he hated getting dressed up even more. He liked his jeans and his favorite shirt and his comfortable sneakers.

That night, a piercing sound awakened Robert. He jumped out of bed, throwing Huckleberry onto the floor with a bump.

"I'm sorry, Huck. What's that sound?"

He couldn't find his slippers in the dark and padded barefoot toward his desk, tripping over the beanbag chair. Groggy, he turned on his desk lamp, almost knocking it over. There it was—his new wrist watch, beeping away. He pressed one button, then another. He couldn't turn it off. He pressed all the buttons at once. At last it stopped.

Grandma Judy was great. But she had sent him the world's worst wrist watch.

No Sleep

Robert slipped his backpack on and went out the front door. He could hardly lift his feet. His wrist watch had gone off three times in the night, each time waking Robert up. He was tempted once to throw it out the window, but because it was from Grandma Judy, he didn't.

He met up with his best friend, Paul, two blocks away. They lived close enough to the school to walk there instead of taking the bus.

Robert told Paul about his birthday.

"Look." He showed Paul his new watch. "You can program it to tell you the time in China. My grandma Judy sent it to me."

"Neat," said Paul.

Paul handed him a small package. "Happy birthday," he said.

Robert took the package and opened it.

It was a key chain with a dog-shaped piece of plastic attached to it.

"I made it out of Sculpy," Paul told him, "but I painted it myself." The dog was a yellow lab with a pink nose. It looked just like Huckleberry.

"Thanks!" Robert said. He took his house key from around his neck, where he wore it on a string for when his parents weren't home after school. He put it on the key chain. A new watch and his own key chain! Robert was feeling more grown up every minute.

Robert got through the morning without falling asleep. He yawned, but he managed to stay awake. The afternoon was another story. That's when they did math.

Math made Robert want to sleep more than anything. His brain seemed to melt down, especially with word problems.

"What is the answer to problem number seven?" asked Mrs. Bernthal. Robert stared at his book and read the problem again. Mary plays the violin, the flute, and the piano. Tim plays the piano and the drums. Jessica plays the clarinet and the flute. How many different instruments do the children play?

It looked easy, but every time Robert thought he had the answer and wrote it down it looked wrong. He erased it four times. Math problems always seemed like trick questions. They made Robert's neck itch. Are the drums considered an instrument? Do you count the piano twice?

Thank goodness Susanne Lee Rodgers raised her hand before Mrs. Bernthal had to call on someone.

"Susanne Lee?" said Mrs. Bernthal.

"They play five different instruments," said Susanne Lee.

"That's right. Did anyone else get it?"

Brian Hoberman raised his hand, and Emily Asher. Maybe Robert wasn't so dumb. A lot of kids didn't get it.

Robert was happy to hear the bell ring, finally. He dragged himself along, talking to Paul on the way home.

"I'm going to a wedding," he said.

"I went to a wedding once," said Paul.

"What was it like?"

"There was a lot of music and everybody danced."

Robert saw people dance to bands like The Rubber Tires in movies. They threw their bodies around in twists and shakes.

"What kind of dancing?" asked Robert.

"I don't know," said Paul. "I don't remember a lot. I was little."

Robert kicked a pebble along as he walked. "I know square dancing from what Mrs. Bernthal taught us."

After finishing *James and the Giant Peach*, Mrs. Bernthal had started reading to them from *Little House on the Prairie*. They had just read about Laura's Pa playing the fiddle at a square dance, so Mrs. Bernthal taught them how to do it. Robert kicked the pebble into the street.

"Hmm," said Paul. "I don't know if they do square dancing at weddings. You may have to learn a regular dance."

Great. He had to wear a suit and a tie and good shoes. And now he had to learn to dance.

Mrs. Crabtree

Robert walked into the room quietly. The old woman looked like she was asleep in her wheelchair. "Mrs. Santini?" he said softly.

Mrs. Santini's eyes opened. "Oh, hello, Robert," she said. "I was just taking a little catnap. Come in."

Mrs. Bernthal brought the class to Sunset Pines Senior Home every month to visit the residents and help them with small errands. Robert liked Mrs. Santini. He always brought her favorite candy bar. Mrs. Santini was old. Robert liked hearing her stories about the old days, just like when Grandma Judy visited.

"Let's go out to the lounge," said Mrs. Santini. "There's more room there." Robert wheeled Mrs. Santini down the hall to the lounge. A couple of people were watching TV. Others were talking or napping.

They chose a sunny spot by the window. Robert sat next to Mrs. Santini in an easy chair. Just as he was about to speak, Robert's new watch went off. *Beep beep! Beep beep! Beep beep!* Robert pressed all the buttons but he couldn't stop it.

Beep beep! Beep beep! Beep beep!

"What is that noise?" shouted a sharp voice not far from them. An old woman on a nearby sofa waved her cane. "Stop that racket!" she cried. "Stop it!"

"I . . . I'm trying," said Robert, trying to punch all the buttons he could. Finally, it stopped.

"I'm sorry," he said. He looked at Mrs. Santini.

"Don't mind Mrs. Crabtree," said Mrs. Santini in a low voice. She patted Robert's hand. "She's an old grouch who complains about everything. She isn't very happy. She'll be all right in a minute."

Robert felt shaky. He explained about the watch. "My Grandma Judy gave it to me for my birthday," he said. "I haven't figured it out yet."

"There are many things I haven't figured out yet," said Mrs. Santini, laughing. "But you're smart," she went on. "You'll get it, one of these days. So you've had a birthday. How old are you?"

"Nine."

Mrs. Santini said nine was a good age. "That was the year I learned to roller skate," she said. Robert couldn't imagine Mrs. Santini ever being nine, and on roller

skates! He remembered to give Mrs.
Santini the Seven Wonders candy bar she
liked.

"That's funny. It's your birthday and
you bring me candy." Mrs. Santini thanked

him and told him, once again, to keep the change from the dollar she had given him.

"How is that puppy of yours?" asked Mrs. Santini.

"He's great," said Robert, smiling. He showed her the key chain with the Sculpy dog that looked like Huckleberry.

"Maybe you can bring me a photograph of him next time you come," said Mrs. Santini.

A woman was just passing by when she stopped. "Excuse me," she said. "I couldn't help overhearing you. I'm Marla, the Recreation Director. I was just thinking about a new program, bringing pets in to visit. Is your dog well behaved?"

"Yes," Robert said. "I trained him myself."

"Elderly people like animals," said Marla, "but many of them can't take care of pets, so visits are good for them. I should talk to your teacher. Perhaps your class could bring in their pets one day."

"Cool," said Robert. He knew Mrs. Santini would love Huckleberry. But he had to laugh thinking about what Mrs. Crabtree would say when she heard about this.

Shopping

Robert dragged his feet as he walked alongside his mom. He hated shopping for clothes even more than he hated getting his hair cut at Ernesto's Emporium. They stopped in front of Boys Will Be Boys. "Let's go in here, Robert."

Robert hung back while his mom went through racks of suits. She picked out a navy blue one.

"Try this on, Rob," she said. A salesman led them to a dressing room.

As Robert took off his pants, his watch went off again. *Beep beep! Beep beep! Beep beep!* Robert frantically tried to stop it. The salesman came running in as Robert smacked his watch.

"Is there a problem?" asked the salesman.

Robert stood there, in his underwear, unable to speak.

Beep beep! Beep beep! Beep beep!

He punched at the buttons. "It's . . . it's . . . O.K.," he said, sounding lame. His face was getting hot. "It's just my watch."

Robert's mom burst in. "What's wrong?" she asked.

"It's his watch," said the salesman.

Beep beep! Beep beep! Beep beep!

Robert grabbed the pants off the hanger and quickly got into them. You never knew who was going to come in next. He put on the jacket and hurried out of the dressing room. The watch was still beeping.

"Let me see," said the salesman. He took Robert's wrist and looked at the watch. He pressed a couple of buttons, and the beeping stopped.

"Thanks," Robert muttered. How did he do that? Robert had pressed all the buttons, and it hadn't stopped for him.

"Don't you look handsome!" said his mom. "You look so grown up, Rob." Robert couldn't care less. He just wanted to go home.

On the way home, Robert sulked in the backseat. This wedding was not turning out to be any fun. First the suit, and now he had to learn to dance. Charlie had told him once he had two left feet. That must mean he didn't dance very well.

If only someone could show him. Susanne Lee Rodgers must know how to

dance—she knew everything. But he couldn't imagine asking Susanne Lee. She made him feel dumb when she helped him. He could ask Kristi Mills, in his class. She took dancing lessons. The thought of asking anyone made his neck itch.

Two Left Feet

On his class's next visit to Sunset Pines, Robert told Mrs. Santini about the wedding.

"A wedding? That's wonderful!" said Mrs. Santini. "I love weddings."

"Everyone dances at weddings, right?" said Robert. If anyone knew, Mrs. Santini would. She must have been to a thousand weddings.

"Yes, of course," said Mrs. Santini. "It's wonderful to dance at somebody's wedding. You're there to wish the couple well and to have a good time."

"What if you don't know how?" Robert asked.

"So you learn," said Mrs. Santini. "It's not so hard."

"I got a book from the library," said Robert, "but I get all mixed up." Robert took a book out of his backpack and showed it to Mrs. Santini.

"Hmm. *You Can Learn to Dance,*" she read.

"It shows where to put your feet with big Xs, but I always forget by the time I go to try it."

"Maybe I can help you," said Mrs. Santini.

Robert wondered how an old woman in a wheelchair could help him, but he didn't say anything.

"Years ago, when I was a girl," said Mrs. Santini, "we learned to dance by making footprints and sticking them to the floor."

"Footprints?" asked Robert.

"Sure. The TV showed us. We watched people dance. Then they showed us footprints on the floor marked 1–2–3–4 so you knew where to put your left foot, your right foot, and then your left foot again. All the young people learned to dance that way. Just follow the footprints."

"That's great," said Robert. It sounded like something he could do.

"Don't worry. You'll learn lots of dances in no time."

"Dances? More than one? I already know how to square dance."

Mrs. Santini laughed. "You'll be fine if you just learn the fox trot. But it doesn't hurt to know a waltz. That's elegant."

"Uh-uh," said Robert. "I don't think so. That's for Prince Charming when he dances at the ball with Cinderella."

"You never know," said Mrs. Santini. "Maybe you will be Prince Charming some day."

Robert smiled. Mrs. Santini was nice, and she meant well. But Prince Charming did not have two left feet.

Footprints

Robert drew a footprint and stared at it. Carefully, he cut out around the heel and toes. The big toe was easy, but the little toes were hard. Robert's hand hurt from holding the scissors tight for so long.

"This is going to take forever," he said out loud. Huckleberry, stretched out on Robert's bed, raised his head.

"Something is wrong," Robert said, looking at the footprint. Of course! Robert wasn't going to dance barefoot. He would have shoes on. The footprint didn't need toes! Huckleberry's head went down again.

Robert took off his sneaker and put it on a clean piece of paper. Then he drew around it with a pencil. There. That was better. He cut out a whole bunch of sneaker prints.

He took off his other sneaker and made footprints from that, too. That was to make sure he didn't have two left feet.

He looked up the dance Mrs. Santini told him about. There it was—the fox trot. Using the Xs in the book as a guide, he put footprints down on the floor and marked them 1, 2, 3, 4, 1, 2, 3, 4. When he finished, he stepped on the footprints, one, two, three, four. It worked. He knew where to put his feet.

When he felt he had it, he plopped down on his beanbag chair to rest. Just out of curiosity, he looked up the waltz. Hmm. Maybe he would try it, just for fun. He needed more room to spread out. This dance took three big steps, making big circles— 1, 2, 3, 1, 2, 3.

Robert put his sneakers on and tied the laces. He picked up the footprints he had cut out, a marker, and the book. He went down the stairs, *thump, thump.* Nobody was home, so he marked the footprints and placed them across the living room floor. One, two, three, one, two, three. He was about to put down another footprint when Huckleberry nudged him.

"Hey, Huck. What's up? You want to go out?"

The big yellow dog wagged his whole body at the word "out."

"O.K." Robert put down the footprints and got the leash. "Come on, boy. We'll take a walk around the block."

When he came back, there were footprints going from the front door up the stairs. Robert followed them. At the top

of the stairs, the footprints went straight up the wall!

Charlie came out of his room laughing. "Yo, Rob!" he cried. "Looks like somebody's been here!" He cracked himself up.

"That's not funny!" Robert shouted, pulling footprints off the wall. They had been stuck on with little pieces of rolled-up tape.

"Oh, lighten up, Rob. It is funny!" said Charlie.

"I was doing something important with these," said Robert.

"You can still do it," said Charlie. "No harm done. You take things too seriously."

"What's going on?" called Robert's dad from downstairs. He must have just come home. "What are all these footprints for?"

Robert hated to tattle, but he couldn't help it. As his father came upstairs, Robert told him what had happened. At first, a little smile crept across his dad's face. Then it disappeared.

"Charlie, you have to have more respect for other people's property," he said. He turned to Robert. "Was anything damaged?" he asked.

"No," Robert said. He was glad his

father stuck up for him. He picked up all the footprints and went to his room. Maybe he'd never learn to dance.

Robert was doodling his gazillionth footprint in his notebook when there was a knock on his door. His mom came in.

"I heard what happened," she said. "Why didn't you ask me for help?"

Robert shrugged. He didn't know his mom knew how to dance.

"Your father and I danced," said his mom. "I was pretty good, if I do say so myself. But your dad had two left feet."

Robert perked up. "Really?" he said.

"Really what? That we danced? Or that your dad had two left feet?"

"Both," said Robert. He laughed.

"Well, you're laughing," said his mom. "That's a good sign. Come on downstairs, and we'll show you something."

Robert and Huckleberry followed her

downstairs. They watched as she put on a CD. She took Robert's dad's hand and started to dance.

They moved this way and that, to the music. "This is the hustle," said Robert's mom. "Everybody danced this in the 70s." Boy. That was a long time ago.

Robert noticed that his dad was a bit clumsy, but his mom kept moving him along. It was great to see his parents in such a good mood. Charlie even came down to watch.

When the music stopped, Robert's mom brushed back some hair that had come loose and changed the CD. This was a bouncier tune.

As the music played, his parents moved to the rhythm. Every now and then they bumped into each other with their hips.

"This one was called the bump," said his mom.

Robert laughed. He couldn't believe how silly his parents looked or that they had ever danced like that.

Afterward, Robert's mom showed him how to do the fox trot to music. At first, it was hard to move his feet without the footprints to guide him, but she made it seem easy.

"Do you know the waltz?" he asked, when they stopped for a rest.

"The waltz? I think so." It took her a while to find a CD to play, but she finally found one.

Robert followed his mom's directions.

"Listen to the music," she said. "And follow my feet. There are three beats. With each one you take another step, making circles as you dance. One, two, three. One, two, three. See?"

They danced around the living room. First square dancing, now circles. It was like math, but with music—and feet.

With his mom leading, he moved around the room, letting the music sink in. A guy with a deep voice was singing about an impossible dream. Robert listened. Yeah. It was an impossible dream all right. Just look at him—he was dancing!

Pet Day

The children filed into Sunset Pines. Marla greeted them. "This is so nice of you, boys and girls. The residents are going to enjoy meeting your pets."

Robert held Huckleberry's leash with his left hand. In his right arm he cradled a small plastic tank holding Fuzzy, his tarantula. Vanessa carried a canary in a wire cage, and Brian Hoberman brought his guinea pig in a shoebox. Susanne Lee had Fluffy, her cat, in a pet carrier. Huckleberry kept sniffing at the little window in the end of the carrier. Fluffy had his eye on the canary.

Marla led the children to the lounge. "May I have your attention, please?" she called. "We have a real treat today. The children from Clover Hill Elementary School have brought in their pets for you to see. You may hold them or pet them if you like. They are all well behaved."

"They have germs!" Mrs. Crabtree shouted.

"The children will come around with their pets," said Marla. "You don't have to touch them if you don't want to. But these are house pets, and they are clean and cared for."

"Don't let them come near me," said Mrs. Crabtree in a cranky voice.

"O.K., children, you may circulate with your pets. You can skip Mrs. Crabtree."

That was a relief. Robert didn't want to go near her anyway.

Robert was on the other end of the lounge with Mr. Steiner, on the leather couch. Huckleberry sat very still and let Mr. Steiner pet him. "Good boy," said Robert. In another moment, Huckleberry had slid to the floor and curled up on Mr. Steiner's feet.

Over by the window, Susanne Lee was placing Fluffy in Mrs. Levine's arms. Mrs. Levine was smiling and petting the soft fur. Fluffy seemed to be enjoying it.

Two old women were reaching into the shoebox to pet Sunflower, Brian's guinea pig.

Robert let Huckleberry stay with Mr. Steiner while he showed Fuzzy to Mrs. Santini.

"Ooooh," said Mrs. Santini. "She's big, isn't she?" She didn't seem to be afraid. "And look at those hairy legs!"

All of a sudden, there was a commotion. "Biscuit! Come back!" Vanessa was crying. Somehow, the canary's cage door had opened, and the bird had escaped. He flew around the lounge, dipping and darting.

"Aieeeee!" squawked Mrs. Crabtree. "Get it out of here! It's going to get in my hair!" Marla ran over to Mrs. Crabtree.

Robert stared. Mrs. Crabtree hardly had any hair.

"Oh, for heaven's sake, Grace," said Mrs. Santini. "It's a little bird. Keep your shirt on."

Marla smiled and hid her mouth with her hand.

Biscuit landed on a curtain rod over the window. Fluffy jumped down from Mrs. Levine's lap and walked slowly toward the window. Uh-oh.

Robert quickly reached for an empty chair. "May I borrow this?" he asked Marla.

"Yes, sure. Take it."

Robert put the chair by the window. He climbed up slowly and carefully, trying not to scare the bird. Biscuit looked around.

Robert talked to Biscuit softly. "Hello, little bird," he said. "You just stay there now. . . ."

Susanne Lee tiptoed up to Fluffy and scooped her up.

Robert kept on talking as he figured out

what to do. Very slowly, he lifted his hand in front of the canary. He put out one finger. The bird watched his hand.

Robert moved his finger a tiny bit closer to the bird. He barely touched the bird's breast. The canary hopped onto Robert's finger. Still talking softly to her, Robert lowered the bird gently.

Vanessa had the cage waiting beside the chair Robert was standing on. Robert bent down and placed his finger right by

the cage door. Biscuit hopped inside. Vanessa shut the little door.

"Hurray for Robert!" said Marla. Everyone clapped, except for Mrs. Crabtree. She just sat with her lips pressed tightly together.

"I'd better go get Huckleberry," said Robert. When he came back, Mrs. Santini was laughing, holding Fuzzy's plastic tank up in front of Mrs. Crabtree.

"Get that thing away from me!" the cranky woman yelled, waving her bony hands to shoo it from her.

Mrs. Bernthal was apologizing to Marla when the director of the nursing home came into the lounge.

Marla greeted him. "Hello, Mr. Strauss."

"Hello, Ms. Edmonds," he said. "I hear there's been a bit of excitement here with Pet Day."

Marla smiled weakly. She had a feather on her skirt. Most of her hair had come undone.

"I always thought we could use more activity here in the afternoons," Mr. Strauss continued. "Maybe we should institute this as a regular thing."

Marla slumped into a chair. Mrs. Bernthal and the children laughed. So did many of the old people. Mrs. Crabtree still had not opened her mouth.

On the way home in the bus, Robert told Paul, "Old people are just like us. There are some bossy ones and some nice ones and some who are afraid of everything, and they even play tricks on each other." Like Charlie. Hmm. Maybe Charlie thought Robert was like Mrs. Crabtree. He sure had to think about that.

The Wedding

The day of the wedding, Robert polished his good shoes. He put on a clean blue shirt, his new suit, and his watch and asked his mom to tie his tie.

As she wrapped one end of the tie around the other and pulled it together, she smiled. "You are incredibly handsome, Rob," she said. Mothers probably had to say that to their kids, but Robert liked hearing it anyway.

He sprayed his hair with stuff that Charlie used and had to admit he looked, and smelled, pretty good. Charlie even whistled a "guy" kind of whistle at him when he walked by.

The wedding was about half an hour's drive from River Edge. Robert rehearsed dance steps in his head, hoping he would remember where to put his feet.

At the synagogue, Robert, Charlie, and their dad were handed white yarmulkes, little skull caps. All the men wore them, even the groom. Up in front there was a canopy draped over four tall columns.

"That's the huppah," said Robert's dad. "The couple gets married under that."

The wedding was kind of long, but Robert amused himself. First, he counted the kids. Seven. Mostly teenagers or little kids.

Then he looked at the grownups. All the men wore suits and ties and had little white yarmulkes on their heads. Robert reached up and felt the one on his head. He must look just like those men, only shorter.

The women reminded Robert of a TV special he had seen on tropical birds. They wore bright colors—royal blue, emerald green, yellow—like jungle parrots. One even had sleeves that looked like wings. His own mother looked like a flamingo in her pink dress.

The bridal party was all dressed up, the women in matching pale blue gowns and the men in tuxedos. Three bridesmaids and three ushers slowly walked up the aisle, followed by a girl around Robert's age, carrying a basket. She had blond hair as curly as Robert's. She dropped rose petals from her basket onto the floor.

Cousin Heather was the last to walk down the aisle. She was dressed all in white with a veil over her head. Her father, Robert's Uncle Stanley, walked with her, his arm in hers.

Under the huppah, the rabbi said some prayers with the bride and groom.

"They're going to break a glass now," Charlie whispered to Robert.

"Who?" said Robert.

"The rabbi."

"Why?"

"I don't know. That's what he does. It's the custom," answered Charlie.

Robert could never be sure whether or not Charlie was teasing him. He kept watching the rabbi.

The rabbi turned to the people and spoke. "If anyone knows of a reason why these two people, Heather and David, should not be married, let them speak now or forever hold their peace."

There wasn't a sound in the synagogue. Then—*beep beep! beep beep!*—a piercing sound filled the silence and everyone turned to look at Robert. Oh no! His watch again! Robert jumped up and ran outside.

After he got the watch quiet again, he couldn't bring himself to go back inside. He wanted to see if the rabbi really broke a glass, like Charlie said he did, but what if his watch went off again?

He found a lounge area and sat down to wait until the wedding was over. He waited so long he went to the bathroom twice and had two paper cups of water at the water cooler.

Finally, the music played and the doors opened, and Heather and David came out, followed by the crowd of people, everyone throwing birdseed. A photographer took pictures as they went down the stairs and into a waiting limousine.

As the girl with the curly hair came out and saw him, she smiled. "See you later," she said.

Robert watched her get into a limousine with others from the wedding party.

It looked like the rest of the day might be a little more interesting than the wedding part.

Lindsey

The first good thing Robert discovered at the reception was that you didn't have to dance if you didn't want to. The band was playing fast music, even some rock-'n'-roll, so the fox trot and the waltz wouldn't work anyway.

Robert looked around and found the flower girl. She was up at the head banquet table with the rest of the wedding party. He was a couple of tables down with his parents and Charlie and several relatives he hardly knew.

"Psst!" Robert looked around. The girl was motioning him to come up to the banquet table. He turned to his mom.

"Is it O.K., Mom?"

She smiled. "Sure. Go ahead."

YES! Robert jumped up and raced across the wooden floor, skidding to a stop next to the banquet table.

"Hi. Come on around," she said. "My name is Lindsey Ilana. What's yours?"

"Robert," said Robert, walking around to Lindsey's side of the table.

Robert sat in an empty chair. The bride and groom and several bridesmaids and their partners were dancing. The rest were sitting at the table, drinking wine and talking.

Lindsey plucked a grape from a fruit bowl and rolled it down the table. Robert grabbed it as it rolled by and popped it in his mouth. Lindsey laughed. Another grape came his way. Robert got that one, too.

As they continued to roll grapes, one of the bridesmaids and an usher came back to the table. A little later, more couples returned. Robert had to give up his chair.

"We can take a walk," said Lindsey, getting up.

Just as they were leaving, one of the bridesmaids cried out, "Oh! My earring!" She clutched at one ear that was empty. "I lost my earring."

"Maybe it's on the floor," said her partner. He bent over to look under the table.

"I'll get it," said Robert. He dove under the banquet table, glad to have a reason to do it. If he was younger, and not so dressed up, he probably would have spent the whole time there.

"I'll help," said Lindsey, crawling under the table with Robert.

On their hands and knees, Robert and Lindsey searched the floor. She went one way, and he went the other.

Finally, by the table leg, he saw something sparkly. It was the earring.

"I got it!" he shouted.

As they crawled back past all the feet, Lindsey giggled.

"What's so funny?" Robert asked.

"Look!" she said, pointing. The bridesmaids had slipped off their shoes and were in their stocking feet. In front of each pair of feet was a pair of shoes. They were all alike.

Robert looked at Lindsey and covered his mouth to keep from laughing out loud. Did she get the idea first or did he? Before he knew it, they had quickly rearranged the shoes so that nobody had the right pair near them.

They came out from under the table
and returned the earring to the bridesmaid. Everyone made a big fuss, especially
the bridesmaid with one earring.

"Thank you!" she said. "You guys are
the best!"

Robert knew if Lindsey giggled, he would burst out laughing, so he said, "That's O.K.," and ran for the back of the hall. Giggling, they watched until one of the bridesmaids got up and tried to slip on her shoes. She said something and another bridesmaid got up. There was confusion and giggling at the banquet table as bridesmaids tried to sort out the shoes. The ushers tried to help, but it got funnier as each bridesmaid kept trying on different shoes until she found the ones that fit.

Robert and Lindsey were laughing so hard, Robert had to hold his stomach. Suddenly, he heard a voice behind him.

"What's so funny?" It was Charlie.

"Charlie!" said Robert, staring at his brother. He swallowed hard. At first, he was going to say, "Nothing." Then he looked at Lindsey, who was still laughing. And he looked over at the banquet table. It was too good to resist. He told Charlie what they had done.

A big grin spread over Charlie's face. "You did that?" he asked. "You played a practical joke on someone?"

Robert nodded.

"Cool!" said his brother.

What do you know, thought Robert. I just impressed my brother.

Prince Charming

Watching from the banquet table as the others danced, Robert looked at his watch. It was blinking, but he had no idea why. He shook his wrist.

"I have the world's worst wrist watch," he told Lindsey. "It goes off when I don't want it to, and now it's started blinking, and I don't know why."

"Let me look at it," said Lindsey.

Robert took off the watch and handed it to her. "Maybe it's broken," he said.

Lindsey played around with the watch for a while and gave it back to him. "It's not broken," she said. "It won't go off again unless you set the alarm."

"What did you do?" he asked.

"I pressed in these two buttons here. That shut off the alarm."

"Great," said Robert. "Thanks." How did she know that? Did girls know everything?

"So why was it blinking?" asked Robert, strapping the watch onto his wrist again.

"Someone must have set it to do that as a reminder of something. I reset it—for 8:32 P.M.—that's right now. When you see it blink next time, you can remember this exact moment, wherever you are and whatever you're doing. Just press the buttons like I showed you to shut it off, if you want."

"No, I like it. I won't shut it off."

Lindsey smiled.

"Ladies and gentlemen," announced the deejay. "This is the final round of dances. We'll be playing a few slow songs as we wind down. When we're ready for our final number, we'll give you a warning, so you can find that someone special to dance it with."

Robert was gazing into space when the music began again. As soon as he heard it, he knew.

"Lindsey, will you dance with me?" he asked.

"I don't know how," she said. He smiled. Maybe girls didn't know everything.

"I can teach you," he said. They went out on the dance floor. Robert showed Lindsey the one, two, three, four pattern. It worked fine, even without footprints to follow.

The next song was a little different.

Robert felt the one, two, three rhythm. "Wow. I can do this, too!" he said.

"You can?" Lindsey looked totally surprised.

"Yeah. Look." He showed Lindsey how to circle, taking one step on each beat— one, two, three, one, two, three. Lindsey was a good learner. She picked it up fast.

As the waltz ended, the deejay announced the very last dance of the evening. "I . . . I'm sorry, but I have to go," said Robert. "I have to do something."

"O.K.," said Lindsey. She looked a little puzzled as she sat down, but Robert knew she would understand.

He walked over to the table where his parents sat. He glanced back at Lindsey. Then he looked at his mom and made a little bow in front of her.

"May I have this dance?" he asked.

"I'd be honored," she replied.

As the music started, Robert and his mom walked out onto the dance floor.

He felt very tall and grown up as their feet began to move to the fox trot.

BARBARA SEULING is the author (and sometimes illustrator) of more than fifty books for children, from picture books and freaky fact books to a guide for adults on how to write for children and several chapter books about Robert Dorfman. She divides her time between New York City and Vermont.

PAUL BREWER likes to draw gross, silly situations, which is why he enjoys working on books about Robert so much. He lives in San Diego, California, with his wife and two daughters. He is the author and illustrator of *You Must Be Joking: Lots of Cool Jokes, Plus 17 1/2 Tips for Remembering, Telling, and Making Up Your Own Jokes.*